Ever Ride a
DINOSAUR?

By SCOTT CORBETT

by SCOTT CORBETT

illustrated by Mircea Vasiliu

New York Chicago San Francisco

Ever Ride a
DINOSAUR?

HOLT, RINEHART AND WINSTON

U. S. 1494781

To BRONSON,
    Wherever He Is

1.

I don't know how you feel about garbage. Personally, I agree with the fellow who said, "I can take it out, or leave it alone." The only trouble was, at my Cousin Charlie's house I seemed to do the taking out and he did the leaving alone.

Whenever his wife, Sarah, wanted the garbage taken out, either Charlie wasn't around, or he had one of his headaches. Charlie was sick a couple of years ago, and he hasn't worked since. The family was worried about how he and Sarah were going to make ends meet, so in a weak-kneed moment I let myself be talked into moving in with them. Their house was close to the bank where I worked as a teller, and the money I paid for board and room would be a lifesaver for them.

So there I was, turning into a general handyman before my own eyes. Since I came, Charlie's health has grown steadily worse, according to his own reports. The doctor says he is much better, but Charlie says the doctor doesn't know what he is talking about. Since I came, Charlie's strength has ebbed to the point where he can't seem to do much of anything around the house any more. "You're so handy about things, Tad," he has often said to me. "I wish I had your gift—and your good health."

Frankly, I have wished for a long time that I could get out of Cousin Charlie's house, but when I have mentioned the fact to anyone in the family they have always said, "Oh, you can't do that, Tad! How would it look for you to walk out on a sick man and rent yourself a place somewhere else with the money he and Sarah need? You couldn't be that selfish!"

For some time now I have had a private name for my room. I call it the Mousetrap.

———————

Charlie's parents, my Uncle Chester and Aunt Lulie, have a place in the country. This weekend we were invited to come down and stay over Saturday night, and nobody was happier to be going than I. This might seem surprising, considering the fact that Uncle Chester is one of the windiest old bores I know of. But it wasn't getting there I looked forward to so much, it was getting *away* once I was there. Away into the woods, for a good long ramble all alone. There is nothing I enjoy more. I can spend hours just watching birds and bees and small animals go about their business.

At such times I always hope nobody else will show up, because it's hard for a grown man to observe nature closely without looking foolish. Take the time I was studying an ant hill. The woods were so still that an interesting idea occurred to me. I thought that if I got down close and listened very carefully, maybe I could hear the scuffle of all those hundreds of ants' feet.

As you might guess, I had hardly got down on my hands and knees when a man and woman came marching along the path.

"What are you doing?" the man asked.

"I'm listening to ants," I said.

They looked at me as if I were crazy.

Well, at any rate, it was Saturday morning, and I was packing my bag and thinking what a fine day it was when I heard the telephone ring. After a while Cousin Charlie came slowly up the stairs. He sank into a chair, panting, and immediately I was worried, because I knew the signs. He always manages to look especially feeble when he's about to ask me to do something unpleasant.

"My, oh, my! I *do* wish I could get my strength back," he said, shaking his head sadly. "Tad, that was Wilson Cates, and he's finally coming to do the plumbing."

Wilson is a grumpy handy man Charlie uses, when he

can get him, because Wilson is cheaper than regular plumbers or carpenters—especially with me helping him. Charlie had been after him for weeks.

"When is he coming?" I asked.

"This afternoon," said Charlie. "He says with you helping him he thinks he can finish up the job by working this afternoon and part of tomorrow. Gee, Tad, I sure hope you won't be too disappointed about having to come back here after you've driven us down to Dad's, but I don't see any other way, do you? You know how hard it is to get hold of Wilson, and he says this is the only free time he has. And after all, you can come down again tomorrow just as soon as you're finished."

———————

I had to drive them to Uncle Chester's because they don't have a car any more. Charlie sold theirs soon after I'd moved in, saying we didn't need two. But one thing I try to do is not let them use my car. The last time Sarah drove it she backed it into another car and cost me a lot of money.

It took better than an hour to drive down, and then I had to turn right around and head home again to the city. It was a fine October day, bright and sunny. I hated the idea of spending it in the basement helping a short-tempered man put in new pipes. Then I began to think about Wilson. He was supposed to show up at one o'clock, but if I knew him he'd be late. I could have an hour's walk and still be home in plenty of time.

I don't know what it was about a certain small side road that came along, but something told me to take it. I turned in and drove along it for a while, and pretty soon I turned off on still another road that was not much more than two tire tracks through the woods. Before long I came out into an open space on top of a hill, near a small woodshed. I decided to leave my car there.

As I stepped out, I saw I was having my usual luck with people. Here came someone. This time it was a little old man, stamping up the slope muttering under his breath. Even though it was such a nice day, crisp but not cold, he had on a great heavy coat that came down almost to his ankles. He looked so peevish that I thought he was going to bawl me out for being on his property.

"Good morning," I said.

"Good, my eye!" he snapped, and shot an angry glance back over his shoulder. "Stubborn so-and-so!"

"What's the matter?"

"Oh, Bronson's making a nuisance of himself!" he said, and shivered so hard he nearly stumbled sideways. "I could freeze to death, for all he cares!"

"Who's Bronson?"

"Friend of mine," he said, and squinted up at me. "What brings you out here?"

5

"I wanted to take a walk in the woods. Is this your property?"

He nodded.

"Some of it," he said, "but if you're foolish enough to tramp around on a miserable cold day like this, go right ahead. Where do you hail from?"

I told him, and one thing led to another. Before I knew it I was telling him my whole story. He seemed to find it interesting. Then all at once he startled me by clapping his hands together and letting out a gleeful chuckle.

"Fixing plumbing! That's no way to spend a weekend like this. Listen here, how would you like to see something really exciting?"

"Well, I don't know," I said cautiously. "What do you have in mind?"

He squinted up at me again.

"Ever see any dinosaur tracks?"

Right about then I decided he must be a crackpot. I didn't know much about dinosaurs, but I did know that most dinosaur tracks in this country have been found preserved in rock in places like South Dakota and New Mexico. Of course, some of those rocks have been taken to museums, but I hadn't heard of any on display in our area.

"Yes," I said, "I've seen dinosaur tracks in museums, but. . . ."

"I don't mean in museums, I mean right where they happened! I mean not half a mile from here!"

Now I was sure he was a crackpot. Because we were in Rhode Island, which is the smallest state in the Union. Why, if you looked at Rhode Island on the map, you would think a full-grown dinosaur could hardly move around there without getting his tail over into Massachusetts or Connecticut, or flipping it into the ocean.

"You mean to say dinosaurs lived around here?" I asked.

He snorted impatiently.

"Certainly! Seventy-five million years ago they did. Dinosaurs lived *everywhere!* They were the most successful creatures that ever existed on the face of the earth. They grew to be the biggest, and they lived on this earth for a hundred million years, which is about ninety-five million more than *men* have been living here."

He glared as if he expected me to say something in favor of human beings, so that he could jump all over me. But I was in no mood to say anything in favor of human beings, so instead I asked a question, just to get away from him.

"Where can I see these dinosaur tracks?" I glanced at my watch. "I don't have much time, but if they're not too far from here. . . ."

He stopped glaring at me.

"Now you're talking sense," he said. "Just you mosey down the hill through that stand of trees till you get to the bottom, then turn due south and keep going till you come to a pond. Won't take you ten minutes. On the edge of the pond you'll see the tracks I'm talking about."

"Well, thank you," I said, not believing a word of it, but figuring I didn't have anything to lose. "I'll go have a look." And I nodded good-by.

I had just turned to walk away when I heard a funny buzzing sound, and a dizzy spell came over me. I had to grab hold of a small tree to steady myself.

"You all right?" asked the old man.

I glanced back at him. He was just putting something in his overcoat pocket.

"Funny, I was dizzy for a second there, but I'm all right now," I said, because already my head had cleared.

"Well, take care," he said, and walked away in the other direction with his coat flapping around his ankles. The way he was cackling to himself, as though he had done something clever, made me feel more than ever that he was some kind of nut.

Even so, curiosity made me keep going in the direction he had suggested. I walked down the hill, worrying about my dizzy spell, and wondering if I had eaten something that disagreed with me. Sarah's fried eggs had been pretty greasy at breakfast. As soon as I got home, I would take some bicarbonate of soda.

It was very quiet in the woods, except for when a rabbit started up and went tearing away into the underbrush. When I reached the bottom of the hill, I could catch a glimpse of water through a gap in the trees. After a couple of minutes I came out of the woods and saw the pond sparkling in the autumn sunshine. It was a small round pond, not two hundred feet across, but with steep banks. There were a lot of water-lily pads floating on it.

I hurried across a meadow and walked over to the edge of the pond. When I reached it, my hair stood on end. There were great big tracks, all right, leading into the water.

The only trouble was, these tracks were in mud, and they were fresh!

———————

Naturally, as soon as the first shock was over, I told myself I couldn't very well be looking at fresh dinosaur tracks.

"What kind of joke does that old coot think he's pulling?" I wondered.

But then the surface of the pond began to heave and bubble like a pot of soup.

Something began to rise up out of the water with the sound of a thousand fat people climbing out of bathtubs.

First a big head on a long neck, then a huge back, and finally part of a great thick tail.

I might not know much about dinosaurs, but I knew one when I saw one.

So I fainted.

2.

Ever have a dinosaur spit water in your face?

When I came to, that was what was happening to me. I looked up into the biggest pair of eyes I had ever seen. The huge creature had lowered his head in my direction at the end of about thirty feet of neck and was making a chuckling sound. He had been spitting water in my face to bring me to. That's the way it seemed, I mean, in this dream I was having—because I was sure it was a dream.

"Good grief!" I cried. "A dinosaur!"

"What did you expect, a catfish?"

"Holy Moses! A talking dinosaur!" I said, and actually felt better. "Well, at least now I *know* I'm only having a bad dream."

He looked insulted.

"Who are you calling a bad dream?"

"Well, I wouldn't call this a good one, when I'm dreaming I'm about to be eaten alive by a dinosaur!"

Now he looked amused.

"Eaten alive? Don't be ridiculous. I'm not one of those meat-eating tyrannosauruses, or anything like that," he said, and closed his eyes with a shudder that rippled the water from bank to bank. "Why, even after all these millions of years I still have bad dreams about *them* myself! So don't talk nonsense. I'm a bronto-saurus, and I don't eat meat—I'm a vegetarian."

Even in a dream, this was good news. But what an amazingly lifelike dream it was—all that part about meeting the old man, and everything! I suddenly re-membered the odd remark the old man had made, the one about a friend of his.

"Next I suppose you'll tell me you're Bronson," I said.

"As a matter of fact, I am. You mean to say Lem said something about me?"

"Lem?"

"My friend Lemuel. The old man you met."

Now I began to feel uneasy. This dream was lasting much too long to suit me.

"This is ridiculous," I said. "You *can't* be real!"

"What do you mean? Listen, I've been real for seventy-five million years now, and that's longer than any other living thing on this earth has been real!"

"Now, look here," I said. I spoke pretty sharply, for me, but then I was annoyed. Even in a dream, when it came to making wild statements, a brontosaurus could only push me just so far. "In the first place, you talk."

"What's wrong with that?"

"Animals can't talk, that's what's wrong with it. In the second place, there haven't been any living dinosaurs for millions of years, so don't stand there in that pond and tell me you're a living, talking dinosaur. I happen to be a modern twentieth-century man with a scientific mind. I don't fall for supernatural stuff or fairy tales."

"You make me laugh," sneered Bronson, sticking his big face close to mine again. "If you really had a scientific mind in that peanut head of yours, you wouldn't be so surprised."

"And why not? Listen, move back and let me sit up, will you?"

"Oh. Sorry." Bronson moved his head back, and I sat up.

"Now, look at it this way," he said. "As Lem probably told you—he tells everybody—we dinosaurs lived over a period of a hundred million years. Doesn't it stand to reason we would develop a few outstanding minds in all that time? I don't like to blow my own horn, but it so happens I'm the smartest dinosaur that ever came along. Know what my IQ is?"

"No."

"Give a guess."

"I wouldn't have the slightest idea."

"What's yours, by the way?"

"Mine? Must be about fifty, or I wouldn't be here," I grumbled.

"No, seriously. Let me see now. . . ." Bronson looked at me keenly. "You're no big brain, that's for sure, but you ought to be good for a hundred and thirty. Maybe a hundred and forty when you're having one of your better days."

"Okay, say mine's a hundred and forty," I agreed, flattered.

"Okay. Well, mine's fifteen hundred."

"Fifteen hundred? That *is* quite an IQ." I had to admit it.

"Your fellows Einstein and Leonardo da Vinci and Shakespeare all rolled together would still be a nitwit by comparison," said Bronson, looking pleased with himself. Modesty was certainly not one of his strong points. "So anyway, with an IQ like that, I was able to figure out quite a few things that are still a little too much for your human minds."

"Such as?"

"Well, such as how to live for more than a hundred years without falling apart, the way you humans do."

Obviously he expected me to believe *anything*. I tried to keep a straight face.

"And how did you manage that?"

"I found out how to change my cell structure in a way that would keep me from growing older."

"No kidding? That almost sounds incredible!" I said, trying to sound very sarcastic.

"Yes, doesn't it?" said Bronson, missing my point entirely. "Of course, in doing so I had to become invisible——"

"In-*what*-able?"

"Invisible. But that has its advantages, too."

I took a deep breath.

"Name one," I demanded.

"Well, I don't suppose I could have survived otherwise. Some of you crazy humans would have figured out a way to hunt me down and kill me by now, I expect."

For a moment I stared up at him. Then I began to laugh. I simply lay back in the grass and began to laugh.

"Man, this takes the cake!" I said, holding my sides. "Now I've got a living, talking, *invisible* dinosaur going for me!"

Bronson snorted again, blowing the grass flat all around me.

"I wish you'd be serious!" he snapped. And when I say snapped, I mean snapped. His jaws came together like some huge steel trap. At a time like that, I could easily imagine them taking a big bite out of something besides a bunch of vegetables. So I decided to stop laughing and humor him a little. Not much, but a little.

"Bronson," I said, "you're going too fast for me. What's this stuff about being invisible? You're no more invisible than I am."

Now he stopped looking annoyed, and even chuckled deep in his throat. Ever hear a dinosaur chuckle? When he chuckles deep in his throat, that's *deep*. Especially a brontosaurus, with all that neck. Sounds like the chuckle is coming out of the bottom of a well. Bronson gave me a sly wink.

"Not invisible, eh? Not to you, I'm not, but that's because Lem gave you a shot with the old Inviso-Ray gun."

"The what?"

"Remember that little dizzy spell you had?"

I stared at him.

"How did you know about that?"

"Oh, we're in constant communication on our own telepathy band. He gave me a full report. He pulled the old Inviso-Ray on you, and——"

"You mean, he fixed it so I can see you?"

"That's right."

"And nobody else can?"

"Well, *he* can, but that's about all. You're lucky. You came along at just the right time. You ought to feel honored. You see, I've been after him for quite a while to take me down to the Museum of Natural History in New York City to look at their dinosaur exhibit, but Lem hates New York City. It's the one place he refuses to set foot in. Well, he's stubborn, and I'm stubborn. Right now it's getting too cold to suit him, here in New England. He wants to start south for the winter. But I've told him I'm not going till I've had my trip to the museum. So he's sitting in his house and I'm sitting here in my pond, trying to wait each other out."

"Why aren't you freezing?" I asked. "That water must be getting cold at this time of year."

"That's true, but since I worked out my new cell setup, I don't notice the cold much. It's a great help."

"You mean to tell me you can live in that water? How do you breathe?"

"Oh, I keep my head out. I was peeking at you all the time from under a water-lily pad."

"But why do you have to hide in a pond if you're invisible?"

"I don't—but don't forget, I wasn't invisible to *you*. And I didn't want you to see me until you were close enough for us to have a chat."

I looked up at him and pretended to be halfway convinced. I shook my head.

"An invisible dinosaur who talks," I said. "An idea like that takes some getting used to."

"But I tell you, it's not all that surprising, when you

think about it. You've been living with all sorts of invisible things all your life. How about radio waves? TV waves? Magnetism?"

"Yes, and they're still invisible. Inviso-Ray gun or no gun, I don't notice any radio waves going by, so far as I can see. I can't see them, I can't feel them. I. . . . Ah-ha!"

Suddenly I knew how to break up my dream. All I had to do was try to feel Bronson!

He seemed to read my mind, because he stuck his big head down at me again.

"Go ahead. Give me a poke in the nose."

"You mean it?"

"Sure."

"No hard feelings?"

"None."

I scrambled happily to my feet. In about ten seconds I was going to be back in my own bed, laughing at this crazy dream I'd had. And in about *twenty* seconds, let me tell you, I would be taking that bicarbonate of soda for my indigestion!

I doubled up my fist and squared off with Bronson.

"You're sure you want me to belt you?"

"Go ahead."

"Okay, you asked for it!"

Of course, I expected my fist to go right through thin air.

Whack!

"Ouch!"

I yelped with pain and danced around massaging my fist while he laughed in a way that was heartless even for a smart aleck brontosaurus. He wasn't even jolted.

"Satisfied?"

"Boy, have you got a hard head!"

"You believe me now?"

It was becoming more difficult not to believe him, but still I didn't. I remembered one time when I was dreaming and pinched myself in my dream to prove I wasn't dreaming, and seemed to feel the pinch in my dream.

"Well, I guess you're there, all right," I said, pretending once more to be convinced, "but I still don't believe you're invisible, if that's what you mean."

He shrugged his shoulders. A brontosaurus shrug is something to see, by the way. The shoulders go up about six feet.

"Well, never mind that for now," he said in a tolerant way, as if now he was humoring *me*. "The big thing at this moment is for us to get our trip organized."

"Our what?"

"Our trip. You see, my problem is an odd one. It's just that the one thing in this life I'm not very good at is direction. My sense of direction is very poor. Why, one time I started to go to— But never mind that now, that was millions of years ago, and come to think of it, it's not even there any more. Ancient history. The point is, if I'm going to get to New York, I'll need help. I told you you're lucky. You came along at just the right time. Lem figured right away that you were the answer to our problem. The old fellow's pretty smart that way."

My spine felt as if someone had plugged it into an electric outlet. This was too much! But then a great new idea occurred to me. Most nightmares end up with someone or something chasing you. You wake up just as you're about to be caught. I braced myself for a scare. This was going to be rough, but it was the only way out.

I pretended to be all for the trip.

"Say, that sounds like quite an experience," I said. But my heart was pounding like a bongo drum. "I've driven to New York, I've taken a bus, and a train, but I've never taken a dinosaur. Tell you what, I've got a road map of Southern New England in my car. I'll just run up and get it. . . ."

And with that, I turned and ran. I started to run with all my might. In fact, I was surprised at how well I did, because you know how it is in a dream, you usually try to run but don't get anywhere.

But as I ran I heard the patter of big, big feet behind me. I hadn't got halfway across the meadow before a push sent me flat on my face. Then I felt a weight holding me down.

Somewhere far above me, Bronson chuckled again.

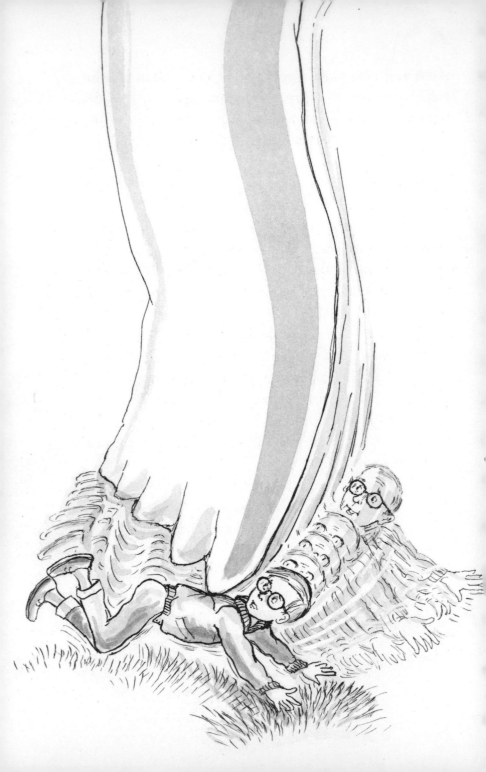

"If that isn't a real dinosaur foot in the small of your back," he said, "it'll do till one comes along."

I had to agree with him there.

"It sure will," I said—and gasped.

Because my voice was as high and shrill as a small boy's!

3.

Bronson took his foot off me. I rolled over and sat up.

"Darn you, now what have you done to my voice?" I yelled. I shook my fist up at him—and then stared at it.

My fist was half its normal size. The mittens my Aunt Betty gave me for my tenth birthday would just about have fit it.

"What—what—?"

"Well, I can't have you trying to run away all the time, so I've shrunk you a little. You're a small boy now, and you'll stay one till we get back. If you ever want to be your old self again, you'd better play ball."

I scrambled to my feet and was amazed to find how

short my legs were. Doing an end run around Bronson, I rushed back to the edge of the pond to look at myself.

When I peered down into the water, a youngster stared up at me.

"Good grief! It's true! I'm a boy!" I cried, and began to blubber.

"Oh, stop sniveling," said Bronson. "What's wrong with being a boy? You'll enjoy the museum just that much more. How many boys do you know who have ever been to a museum with a dinosaur?"

Now that it was too late, now that I had gone too far and gotten myself into a terrible fix, I finally faced the fact that this was no dream I was in. Bronson was really there, and I was really here—what was left of me, that is!

"Don't worry," said Bronson, "it's just for a little while, and when we get back, if you've been a good boy, I'll unshrink you."

Hearing that made me feel better, but hardly solved all my problems.

"Bronson, you don't understand," I said. "I can't go running off to New York with you, I have to go home and help a man work on the plumbing."

"Who says so?"

"Why—er. . . ."

"Look, you're a grown man——"

"Not any more!" I pointed out bitterly.

25

"Well, anyway, you were. So forget about the plumbing. You've got something better to do."

Well, the wonder of what was happening began to come through to me, and I could not help but see his point. Here I was, mixed up with one of the greatest scientific marvels of all times! Was I going to worry about Cousin Charlie and his plumbing at a moment like this?

"Gee, I don't know. Wilson Cate is going to be as mad as a wet hen when he shows up at the house and nobody's home," I said. "And what will I tell Charlie? How will I ever explain where I've been?"

"Don't. Tell him that where you spent your time is none of his business. Live for today! That's what I've been doing for millions of years, and I've never regretted it."

"Well. . . ." I fished around in my pockets for a handkerchief to dry my eyes with. When I unfolded it, it was about six inches square.

"Hey, look what you've done to my handkerchief!" Then I pulled out my wallet. "And look at this! What happens if I get hungry and want to buy a hamburger?"

For once Bronson had the decency to look sheepish.

"I forgot about your wallet. However, it's a mere detail. Lay it on the grass there, and I'll bring it back to full size."

I laid the dollar bill on the grass.

"No, not just that, silly, the whole wallet," said Bronson, and this time I felt foolish. I put the bill back in its place and laid the wallet on the grass. Bronson put his foot over it, and when he took it away again the wallet was normal size. I was examining some of the bills in it when suddenly a new voice made me jump.

"Hey, kid!"

I looked up, and there on the other side of the meadow stood a man. He had small, bloodshot eyes and a big red nose—a bad combination—and his clothes had not been cleaned and pressed for a long time. He looked like a tramp.

He leered at me in a very nasty way.

"What's that you got there, sonny?" he asked in a rough voice.

"What business is that of yours?" I asked, forgetting about my size.

"What business is that of yours?" he said, mimicking my high voice. He walked toward me with his fingers twitching greedily. "That there happens to be my wallet, that's what. Hand it over!"

I looked around at Bronson, bewildered. Was he truly invisible, after all? If this tramp had been able to see what I saw, he would either have started running or dropped dead, or both. But Bronson merely looked amused.

"No, he can't see me or hear me," he said, reading my mind again. "Stick out your tongue at him, and then run. Run and hide behind my left hind leg."

There wasn't time to argue, so I stuck my tongue out and ran.

"You little so-and-so!" yelled the tramp, and came after me as hard as he could go. I ducked behind Bronson's left hind leg and peered around it, scared stiff, as the tramp came at me with one hand out to grab me and the other doubled into a fist.

SPLAT!

He ran straight into Bronson's leg, bounced back off it like a tennis ball, and sprawled on his back on the ground. He was out cold. Bronson's big head swung around at me on its long neck. He was positively grinning.

"*Now* do you believe I'm invisible?"

I stared down at the tramp.

"Now I'll believe anything," I admitted.

"Good. Then let's go."

Bronson stepped delicately over the unconscious man, and we started across the meadow.

"I'll tell you one thing," I said, looking back, "I'd like to watch his face when he wakes up and sees those tracks of yours. . . ."

"Oh, use your head! What kind of tracks would an invisible dinosaur leave?"

"I suppose now you're going to tell me——"

"Right! Invisible tracks. If that man can't see me, he can't see my tracks, either."

"But what's he going to think when he wakes up?"

"He's going to think he ran into a small boy with the greatest karate chop in the world," said Bronson.

Well, even as worried as I was, I couldn't help chuckling at that. And all at once I felt like a different man—or boy, I should say. Up to now my life had not exactly been an exciting one. Now I was making up for it with the greatest adventure I could ever have imagined!

"Bronson, even if you turn me back into a middle-aged man now, I won't run away," I said. "This is amazing!"

"I think I'll keep you a small boy," said Bronson. "I like you better that way."

I shrugged—a small, three-inch shrug.

"Well, I don't care. It's an experience," I said. We grownups often sit around talking about how much we'd like to be boys again. Well, now I *was* one, and it was a marvelous feeling. I felt light and springy. It was astounding how much energy I seemed to have.

"It's an experience," I said again.

We walked through the woods, with Bronson brushing the treetops aside, and reached the woodshed, where my small red station wagon was waiting.

"Say, what are we going to do with my car?" I asked. "I can't leave it standing here all weekend. Especially not with that tramp around."

"Well, let's put it in the woodshed."

I gave him a look. My car was small, but not that small, not by a long shot.

"Bronson, that fifteen hundred IQ of yours must be slipping, if you can't see that it's too big to go in there."

"I'll fix that," said Bronson. "But first you'd better take out the road map. No point in having it too small to read."

"You mean—?"

"Yes."

"This I've got to see," I said.

I opened the car door and took out the map. Then Bronson lifted his right front foot and rested it on the roof.

"Take it easy, now! I don't want any dents in that car! I haven't even finished the payments on it yet."

"Don't worry."

And as I watched, my station wagon shrunk down to a toy car about eight feet long. I'll be perfectly honest with you. It was one of the most unusual sights I have ever watched.

"Okay, now get out your car keys," said Bronson. "They ought to fit."

I took out my key ring and saw that my car key was half its normal size. I had forgotten about having it in my pocket. When I tried it, the key fit perfectly.

I wish every boy could have a toy car like that miniature station wagon. It was terrific.

"Let me drive this thing around a little, Bronson," I said. "This is great!"

"All right," he said. "I'll be nosing the shed door open while you take a spin, but don't be long."

He chuckled that superior chuckle of his again.

"I know you won't try to get away," he said. "You wouldn't go ten blocks before some cop would make you pull over. And remember, you don't match the description on your driver's license very well any more. I'm glad you wore those clothes, by the way," he added. I had on a field jacket, plaid wool shirt, tan slacks, and sneakers. "They don't look much different from what a lot of boys wear these days."

I drove down the road a way and nearly tipped over my new mini-wagon turning it around, because of the high crown of the road. When I got back, Bronson had the door of the woodshed open. I drove the car inside. There was plenty of room. But I was still worried.

"What about that tramp? If he comes up here, he may break in."

"I'll fix that," said Bronson, glancing around. Our part of New England is full of glacial boulders left by the last Ice Age. He found a big one, and nosed it over against the shed door.

"That ought to take care of things," I admitted.

We looked at each other. Then I looked at my watch. It was a good deal smaller than I was used to, but I could read it without difficulty. My eyesight

seemed to be much keener than it used to be, and I wasn't even using my reading glasses.

"Well, it's nearly noon," I said. "If we're going to reach New York City in time to visit the museum, we'd better get started!"

U. S. 1494781

4.

Ever ride a dinosaur?

The best way to mount a brontosaurus is to climb up his tail. The slope is not too steep, and the scaly hide is rough enough to give good footing. Even so, sneakers or other rubber-soled shoes are advisable. Never wear shoes with slippery leather soles when planning to ride a brontosaurus.

I was not able to put a tape measure on him, but I would say Bronson went a good seventy feet from head to tail. He had three claws on each hind foot, and one claw on each fore foot. For his size, his head was small, but that still made it big.

When I got up on his back I took a walk around, looking it over.

"How am I supposed to stay up here?" I asked. "There's nothing to hold onto."

"What do you expect me to do, grow you a seat belt? You'll manage fine. Just sit down, and we'll go for a trial spin."

"Well . . . all right." I sat down cautiously in the middle of his back.

"All set?"

"Yes."

"Here we go!"

It is impossible to describe the way it felt when all that seventy feet of dinosaur began to move. I was bouncing around up there like popcorn in a popper.

"Hey! Stop!" I yelled, flopping around and grabbing for handholds.

"Wait till I hit my stride," said Bronson over his shoulder. "Then things will smooth out."

Sure enough, he began to get his big feet working together, and I settled down in one place.

"How's that?" he said. "You couldn't get a better ride than that on the best railroad in the country."

He was right. After a while I even lolled over on one elbow as I watched the scenery roll by. But then a crazy thought made me sit up.

"Hey, wait a minute! Nobody can see *you*, but how am *I* going to look, sailing along thirty feet off the ground? Talk about Unidentified Flying Objects, I'll

36

be lucky if some Nervous Nellie doesn't shoot me down!"

"Relax," said Bronson, chugging along. "The instant you stepped aboard, you picked up my invisibility."

He really shook me with that piece of news. It was the worst shock yet.

"What? Me, invisible?"

I was so scared I began to bawl again.

"*Now* what are you sniveling about?" asked Bronson.

"I don't want to be invisible!"

"Oh, stop it," he said. "There's nothing to it, once you get used to the idea. Besides, you'll only stay invisible as long as we're in contact."

I choked back a sob.

"Are you sure?"

Bronson sighed, blowing leaves off several passing trees.

"Can't you take my word for *anything?*" he asked.

We had come down a hill through a patch of woods to the edge of an open field. On the far side of it was a farmhouse. An old farmer was busy in the side yard, sorting apples into baskets.

"We'll stop behind that old fellow sorting apples into baskets," said Bronson, "and you get off and ask him a question."

He clomped across the field. I climbed backward down his tail and stood clear.

"Hello, mister," I said. "What are you doing?"

The old farmer gave me a brief glance over his shoulder.

"What does it look like, sonny?" he snapped. "I'm sorting apples into baskets."

He never knew how good he made me feel. I all but danced up Bronson's tail again. By that time the farmer had thought to wonder about me. He glanced over his shoulder again. Then he straightened up for a good look around.

"What the dickens . . . ? Where did that young'un come from—and where did he go?"

"Here I am!" I shouted, testing him. But he didn't even glance my way. I was convinced. He could neither see nor hear me. I kicked my heels against Bronson.

"Giddap, boy!" I said. "Let's go!"

Bronson gave me a cold look as he moved off.

"We can dispense with that 'giddap' stuff," he suggested. "Save that for your next pony ride."

"Sorry, Bronson. I was feeling good, that's all."

"Maybe next time you'll believe somebody when somebody tells you something," he said, still being uppity. "Now get busy with that road map and figure out where we're going. We'll keep off the highways —I'm not about to have a bunch of sports cars whizzing between my legs—but our best bet is probably to stay parallel to the main routes, so we'll know where we are."

I studied the road map for a moment, while Bronson was jogging down a hill.

"Okay, take a left," I said. "We'll head south and stay alongside the turnpike on the other side of the state forest. That's the best way to get to New York from here."

"And when we get to the turnpike, do I take another left, or a right?"

"Say, you *do* have a poor sense of direction, don't you? You take a right, of course."

Bronson snickered. Pacing himself nicely now, he trotted through the state forest, which was pleasant at that time of day, and absolutely deserted. We didn't see another soul.

"Lots of Indians used to live around here, a few years ago," remarked Bronson. "Three or four centuries ago, that is. They were a nice bunch, those Indians. If you ask me, they ran a better country than you people do. Why, there are streams and ponds around here I wouldn't think of going into today, and most of your air isn't fit to breathe. It beats me how Lem stands it. As I've said to him more than once, it was a sad day for this continent when those Pilgrim Fathers of yours set foot on it."

I didn't feel like getting into an argument with

Bronson about America the Beautiful, so I decided to satisfy my curiosity instead.

"Did they really step ashore on Plymouth Rock?" I asked.

I hate to say so, but he snorted cynically.

"No, that's just a story," he said. "They simply rowed ashore and hopped out onto the beach like anybody else."

About then we came out of the state forest and were close to the highway. I saw a roadside restaurant, and all at once I was so hungry my mouth was watering.

"Hey, how about a rest stop?" I said. "I want a hot dog."

"I could use a breather," admitted Bronson, and pulled up. "Go ahead."

"You want anything?"

"I seldom eat," he said. "Don't have to, with this new cell setup of mine."

"Well, with this new cell setup of *mine*, I've suddenly got an appetite," I said as I slid down his tail. "I haven't been this hungry since the last time I was a boy."

I ordered two hot dogs and a double-scoop chocolate ice-cream cone. When I took out my wallet to pay, the woman at the cash register could see I had quite a few bills in it, about ten dollars in all. She gave me a funny look, but didn't say anything. When I went out, though, I heard her sniff and say to a friend, "These spoiled kids today have too much money."

Bronson was amused when he saw all I had bought.

"That ought to hold you for a while, sonny," he said. "Okay, all aboard!"

I was gaining more confidence now. This time, what with having my hands full, I walked up Bronson's tail the way you would walk a log, and made it very nicely.

"Okay, take a right and follow the highway," I said, and settled down to my feast.

It was quite an experience to sit there licking my ice-cream cone and look over at the cars on the highway and see people staring out of them straight at us with a bored expression. If they could have seen what was running along beside them, there would have been a lot of cars whizzing off into the ditches.

"By the way," said Bronson, "what's your name?"

I told him it was Thaddeus Marsh, Tad for short. He asked me where I lived, and I told him all about that.

"Well, I agree with Lem," he said, "you shouldn't spend a day like this messing around with someone else's plumbing. You know, if you don't mind my saying so, that cousin of yours sounds like a phony."

"Yes, but I'm stuck with him. If I moved out and got a place of my own, the whole family would be down on me. How would he and Sarah get by?"

"Hmm. From what I've seen of human beings, people like your Cousin Charlie always get by. However, I guess he's your problem, Tad."

We had not gone far before we crossed the state line into Connecticut.

"Connecticut!" said Bronson. "Say, that reminds me. Connecticut raises a lot of tobacco, you know."

"I know," I said, wondering why he would bring up a thing like that. "There's quite a few tobacco farms down through here."

"That's right. By golly, I could use a good cigar along about now."

I was amazed.

"You mean to say you smoke?"

"Why, sure. I've been smoking for about twenty thousand years."

I shook my head sadly.

"That would certainly be a blow to people who say smoking is a bad habit," I said.

"Listen, I wouldn't *think* of smoking cigarettes," Bronson assured me. "But a cigar now and then is another story, especially if you don't inhale. If you human beings would only stick to cigars, and not inhale, you'd be a lot better off. Do you smoke, Tad?"

"No, I gave up cigarettes years ago. But listen, why didn't you say something back at the restaurant? They had cigars. I'd have been glad to treat you to some."

Then I remembered my condition, and laughed.

44

"What am I saying? I'm a boy! I can imagine that woman's face if I'd stepped up and said, 'Hey, lady, let me have a couple of those big Corona cigars.' "

"Never mind, they wouldn't do me any good, anyway. They may look big to you, but I couldn't even light one of them without burning my nose. I need something more suitable to my size. Actually, I've always rolled my own, out of full-sized tobacco leaves. That's what started me thinking about Connecticut tobacco farms. If we could find a tobacco barn where they've got some leaves hanging up, drying. . . ."

"Now, wait a minute! We can't go——"

"Let's look around," he said, and there wasn't a thing I could do about it. Bronson had his mind set on a cigar.

5.

It was astonishing how soon Bronson found his way to a tobacco farm, once he decided to look for one. When he wanted something, his sense of direction seemed to improve remarkably.

"I thought I remembered it right," he said, when he had sighted the broad, flat fields of a tobacco farm, with the drying sheds along one side. "This is a good farm, too. Raises a very decent brand of tobacco."

"How come you found your way to it so easily?" I asked. "I think all this talk about your sense of direction is a lot of malarkey!"

Bronson snickered again.

"It's no fun going to museums alone," he said. "I like company."

46

I drummed my heels angrily on his back.

"You big faker! Now I know why you were snickering a while ago! You pulled me into this deal on false pretenses!"

His head swung around, and an enormous eye twinkled at me.

"Well, you wouldn't have missed it, would you?"

I looked away grumpily, but I had to be fair about it.

"No, I suppose not," I admitted. "I haven't had a weekend like this in years."

"You bet your life you haven't. Well, now, let's have a look in one of those barns."

Bronson trotted straight across the fields—nothing was growing at that time of year. He poked his head into a shed through a big open door. Down at the other end of the shed a couple of men were looking at some of the tobacco leaves that were hanging from poles strung the whole length of the barn.

"I'll wait till their backs are turned," said Bronson. "It might disturb them if they saw a tobacco leaf suddenly disappear into thin air."

"You mean, when you touch it . . . ?"

"That's right. It will become invisible."

Bronson was picky. He didn't take the first leaf he saw. He sniffed several, and looked them over carefully, before he made his selection. Then he waited for his chance, and neatly stripped the leaf off its pole. It

47

was a big leaf, about two feet across. He laid it on the ground, turned in one edge with his mouth, rolled the leaf neatly together with his chin, and licked it along the edge, like somebody rolling a cigarette. With one end of it in his mouth, he straightened up and swung his head around, this way and that, surveying the landscape. In the distance a curl of smoke could be seen.

"Ah! Somebody's burning leaves," he said. "That ought to do it."

He trotted over in that direction and found a man standing by a pile of leaves. But they were only smoldering. They were giving off lots of smoke, but no fire. The man was coughing and swearing.

"Come on, burn!" he said impatiently, and raked them together. Bronson laid his cigar down out of sight behind a bush. He lowered his head to the ground near the base of the pile and blew.

"Phoo! Phoo!" went Bronson, while the man looked surprised that a breeze had suddenly sprung up. The pile began to blaze. Bronson picked up his cigar, lighted it, and strolled away. I looked back at the man. He had wet a finger and was holding it up, trying to figure out which way the wind was coming from.

"Not bad," said Bronson, puffing on his cigar. He jogged along contentedly, heading back toward the highway. He had to talk out of the side of his mouth while he was smoking, but he managed that very well. "I'll tell you a funny story about tobacco.

You've heard the expression, 'Once in a blue moon,' I suppose. Well, a blue moon only comes along once every ten thousand years. That's the reason for the expression."

"That's very interesting, Bronson," I said. "I didn't know that."

"I've made quite a study of these things," he said. "But anyway, the point of my story is that ordinary human beings can see me once in a blue moon, so it's a touchy time for me. I generally go into hiding for the night. Now, tobacco used to grow wild in several parts of the world, and one of the best patches in those days was in China, near a place called Woo Chu. That year I was hanging around Woo Chu, making the most of that patch, and I forgot all about the blue moon. When you get to be my age, ten thousand years goes by like nothing."

"I can imagine," I said.

"Yes, time really flies. But anyway, I was sitting up on a hillside in the blue moonlight, enjoying a cigar, when along came a bunch of Chinese villagers, heading home from a wedding. They looked up and saw me sitting there with smoke rolling out of my nostrils—and that was the beginning of the legend of dragons. You should have seen that wedding party take off in all directions! That's how all the talk about dragons got started. *I* started it. The Chinese have a different name for each year, you know—twelve names, and then they begin again. There's the Year of the Rat, the Monkey, the Horse, the Tiger, and so on. Well, that was the first Year of the Dragon."

Bronson blew a big cloud of smoke out through his nostrils and looked pleased with himself.

"You know what I think, Bronson?" I said. "I don't believe you forgot about the blue moon at all. I think you did that on purpose."

He snickered guiltily.

"You're pretty sharp," he said. "As a matter of fact, I did. I was a great practical joker in those days."

"If you ask me, you haven't changed much," I grumbled, and that made him snicker all the more.

We were back alongside the highway, and making good time, when Bronson began to wiggle his back around.

"What's the matter?" I asked.

He stopped.

"My back itches."

"Where? I'll scratch it."

"Ha! You don't think those dinky fingernails of yours would do me any good, do you?" he said, and his neck was swinging like a crane as he looked around, this way and that. "Let me see, now. . . ."

"What are you looking for?"

"Ah!" said Bronson, and trotted off toward a house where another man was burning leaves in his back yard. His wife was on her hands and knees in the side yard, digging in a flower bed. A rake was leaning against the house in the back yard.

Bronson had just about finished his smoke, so he dropped his cigar butt and stamped on it, putting it out. Then he walked over, took the rake in his mouth, and lifted it up to me.

"Here, use this."

"Where does it itch?"

"Just below my right shoulder," said Bronson. I went to work raking his back in that vicinity.

"How's that?"

"A little lower. Now to the left a little. Higher! Now just a hair to the left. Ah-h! That's it! Keep it up!"

Meanwhile the man burning leaves turned and reached for his rake. When he saw it wasn't there, he went stomping around the side of the house to his wife.

"Listen, I wish you'd get your own rake, instead of taking mine!" he barked at her.

She glared up at him.

"I didn't take your rake."

"What do you mean, you didn't take it? It's gone!"

"I don't care, I didn't take it."

"I suppose it just walked away!"

"It must have fallen down."

"Fallen down, nothing! I tell you, it isn't there!"

With a big sigh, the man's wife stood up.

"Let's just see," she said.

"Quick, hand me the rake," said Bronson, and I handed it back to him. He leaned it against the house again just before the man and his wife came around the corner, still arguing.

We didn't wait to see how the poor fellow got out of that one. Bronson trotted away briskly, and when I looked back there was a lot of arm-waving going on.

"Bronson," I said, trying not to laugh, "you're the world's biggest rat."

"Don't talk about me. You were in an awful hurry to hand me that rake in time to put it back before they got there," said Bronson.

I had to admit I was as guilty as he was.

"I hate practical jokes," I said, "except when they're mine."

"That goes for most practical jokers," said Bronson.

"I'm afraid so," I agreed. "For instance, I'll never forget one time when I was crouched down in the woods admiring a butterfly sitting on a blade of grass when I heard some bird watchers coming."

"Those bird watchers," said Bronson, chuckling. "I get a kick out of watching *them* sometimes."

"So do I. There's two kinds, you know. There's the kind who move carefully and silently, and the kind who talk all the time and wonder why they don't see more birds. These were the second kind. Two women. Well, the soil was sandy where I was kneeling, so I drew a wavy line in it with my finger and waited. Pretty soon they came along.

" 'Good morning!' said one of them. 'What are you looking at?'

"I pointed to the wavy line.

" 'Something you don't see very often,' I said. 'Fresh rattlesnake tracks!' "

Bronson laughed.

"I'll bet that got rid of *them* in a hurry!"

"They made a few tracks themselves," I admitted.

"Pretty good," said Bronson. "But you take that rake trick, now, that reminds me of the cherry tree joke I pulled once on your first president."

"Who? You mean George Washington?"

"Who else? I can tell you, your history books got that cherry tree story all wrong. The way the books tell it, young George chopped down a cherry tree, and then when his father wanted to know who had done it, he said, 'I cannot tell a lie. I did it.' Well, that's not the way it happened at all. Actually, what happened was this, and I know, because I was hanging around the orchard at the time. There was this old dead cherry tree, you see, and his father said, 'George, that tree ought to come down. Take this hatchet and chop it down for me. The exercise will do you good.'

"So Mr. Washington went back in the house, and George got to work. He chopped it down, and then ran in the house to tell his father he'd finished the job.

"As soon as he'd left, I pulled out the stump and stuck the cherry tree back in the ground and stamped the dirt down around it so carefully you'd never know it had been touched.

"Pretty soon here came Mr. Washington and son George to have a look. Well, I wish you could have seen that boy's face when he saw the cherry tree still standing there. His father was annoyed.

" 'George, I'm getting tired of your silly jokes,' he said. 'Now you get busy and cut down that tree or I'll fan your britches!'

" 'But, Father, I *did* chop it down!' said George.

" 'You what? I'll teach you to tell a lie!' said Mr. Washington, and with that he turned George over his knee. Then he stamped back into the house, leaving poor George rubbing his bottom and glaring at the tree.

" 'Darn old tree!' said George, and gave it a good kick.

"Naturally it fell right on over. George stared at it for a moment. Then he turned and ran for the house.

" 'Hey, Pop, guess what happened!' he yelled. As soon as he was gone I stuck the tree back in the ground *again*, and then I left."

Bronson snickered wickedly.

"I just couldn't stand to see what happened when George brought his father out the *second* time."

"Bronson, you're a menace!" I said.

"Oh, you have to have a little fun once in a while in this life," he said. "But speaking of jokes, now that the truth is out about my sense of direction, we might as well head across country instead of following the highway. Actually, we can take a short cut or two and make better time. And besides that, the scenery will be nicer."

"Good idea. Let her roll," I said, and sprawled out comfortably to watch the world go by. One amazing thing about us human beings is how quickly we can get used to *anything*. One minute a new invention is the greatest marvel of all times. The next minute, we're taking it for granted. That's the way I was about riding on Bronson. After a while it didn't seem much different from looking out of a train window and seeing a lot of people go by who were busy with their own affairs and not paying any attention to me. After all, a person might as well be invisible on a train, for all anybody really sees of him as he goes past.

As a cross-country runner, Bronson made it look easy. He could step over the highest fence or wall we came to without even breaking his stride. Most of the roads we crossed were side roads without too much traffic on them, though I must say, he was careful. He always looked both ways before crossing. Once in a while we came to a small stream, but nothing he couldn't wade without so much as getting his belly wet.

Everything was fine until we topped a ridge and I saw something below us that gave me a jolt. I was so used to driving down to New York and crossing a couple of big bridges along the way that I had forgotten all about why the bridges were there.

They were there because of a couple of big, wide rivers, and one of those rivers was ahead of us now.

"Bronson!" I said. "How are we going to get across?"

6.

Bronson gave me a nonchalant look.

"Are you kidding?" he said. "Why, normally we brontosauruses spent most of our time in the water, keeping our weight off our legs. Believe me, I wouldn't be running around this much if it weren't for my new cell setup. To be honest about it, I've got to admit that your average brontosaurus was on the sluggish side. He never moved very fast or very far unless a tyrannosaurus was chasing him. *Then* he could get up and go, don't think he couldn't. But otherwise he was usually found nibbling on shrubs and trees and grasses near some swampy spot, and when he wasn't eating he was up to his neck in water, letting the water hold him up and take the weight off his feet. Swimming is a cinch for us. Why, that little river down there is nothing. You should have seen me swimming the Mississippi. And I'm not talking about that little trickle you've got today. I'm talking about the *old* Mississippi, back in the days when it was a thousand miles wide."

I listened to all this with as much patience as I could manage. At another time I would have been more interested, but at the moment I had more pressing matters to think of, such as self-preservation.

"That's all very well," I said, "but how am *I* supposed to get across?"

To give Bronson credit, he did see my point at once.

"Hmm," he said. "You've got something there. What with the current and all, there's liable to be a little wash breaking across my back now and then. . . ."

"You're darn right there is," I said, "and I'm not anxious to get soaked to the skin at this time of year. I'd catch my death of cold!"

Bronson pawed the ground in an annoyed way. He was vexed with himself.

"I should have thought of this," he admitted. "Well, we'll just have to go downstream a few miles to the nearest bridge, where you can get across."

We were not even halfway to New York City yet. I looked at my watch.

"That's fine, but if we waste much more time we'll never make it to the museum before closing time."

"Oh, that!" Bronson tossed his head in a carefree manner. "I never figured we'd make it anyway. What we'll do is, we'll spend the night in the park and go over in the morning, when we're fresh."

I stared at him.

"What park?" I cried. "Do you mean Central Park?"

"That's right," said Bronson. "I understand the museum is just across the street from Central Park."

"Now, wait a minute!" I said, pounding my small fist on his back. "You never said anything about being away overnight!"

"Well, now, Tad, be reasonable——"

"Reasonable my foot!"

"Look at it this way. You've blown the plumbing job anyway, so you might as well stay away all weekend."

He was right about that, of course. I wasn't anxious to face Cousin Charlie and Wilson Cates. Still. . . .

"But how do you expect me to sleep in a park at this time of year?" I said. "I'll freeze!"

Bronson chuckled heartlessly.

"Okay, walk into a hotel and ask for a room. Maybe you'll get away with it. Maybe they'll think you're a midget."

"Now, listen, Bronson," I said, "fun's fun, but I am not going to——"

"Oh, relax! We'll stop somewhere and you can buy yourself a sleeping bag. What kind of kid are you, anyway? Most kids would love the idea of camping out with a real live dinosaur in Central Park. We'll gather twigs and build a campfire and toast marshmallows. We'll have a ball!"

It was the marshmallows that got me. *I* was not sold yet, but my ten-year-old stomach loved the idea.

"Well. . . ." I said, weakening.

"Come on! Live it up! Have some fun out of life! Good grief, if I worried as much as you do, I'd have been dead millions of years ago!"

And you know, he was right. Suddenly I saw that. Camping out in Central Park, sitting around a campfire with a dinosaur, and then snuggling down in a sleeping bag for a night in the open—what could beat that?

"Bronson, you win," I said. "We human beings do worry too much. Your idea sounds great!"

"Now you're talking," said Bronson, and we jogged along for a while in a companionable silence, better friends than we had been before.

A few minutes later we had to stop to let a train go by.

"I never see a string of freight cars rolling along,"

said Bronson, "but what I'm reminded of the time I invented the wheel."

"What? The wheel?" Naturally I was skeptical. "Why, the wheel is supposed to be one of primitive man's greatest inventions, if not his greatest."

"Maybe so," said Bronson, "but let me tell you what happened."

"I'd like to hear about it," I said.

"Well, there were these four cavemen, and were they dumb!" began Bronson. "This was quite a while ago. They had learned to make pots out of clay, but that's about all you could say for them. They used to go down to a river and dig clay along the banks. They piled the clay on a mat their women had woven out of straw and dragged it back up the slope to their caves. It was hard going, and what's more, the straw mats wore out in no time. I used to watch those poor fatheads and say to myself, there *must* be a better way to move a heavy load than that!

"So I started thinking about it. Right away I thought, 'Roll it!' but it took me a while to think of a way to *keep* rolling it. Finally I got my big idea. Wheels! Now the only problem was, how to get some wheels made up for me. Then I remembered there was a beaver colony a couple of miles up the river.

"Beavers grew big in those days. They didn't fool

around with trees less than four feet in diameter, and I figured four feet would make a nice-sized wheel. So I went to the head beaver and said, 'Listen, I want you fellows to——' "

"Now, wait a minute, Bronson," I said. "Just wait a minute. Are you claiming you can talk to beavers?"

"Certainly," he said. "Not only can I speak over eight hundred of your human languages, I can also speak horse, dog, cat, kangaroo, elephant, beaver—well, you name it. Aardvark? I speak fluent aardvark. But anyway, I said to the head beaver, 'Listen, I want you fellows to gnaw me out a set of wheels.'

" 'Wheels?' says he, 'what's wheels?'

" 'It's an idea I'm working on,' I said. 'What I want is a couple of flat slabs of tree trunk with holes in the middle I can stick a sapling through.'

" 'Sounds crazy to me,' he said, but at the same time he was interested. He called over some young beavers and put them to work, and in no time at all I had my wheels. But of course wheels are nothing without an axle. It was my invention of the axle that I was almost more proud of than anything. I had them gnaw me off a ten-foot length of nice, straight sapling, and I stuck one wheel on each end, and was ready to make history. Or so I thought, anyway.

"I went back down river to where the four cavemen were gathering clay and got up on top of the slope above them. When they started up, dragging a load of

clay, I pushed the set of wheels over the edge of the slope and let it roll down toward them. I figured they couldn't help but get the idea.

"Now, the oldest man among them was called the Wise Man, and the youngest was called the Wise Guy. When they saw the wheels coming, they stopped to watch. They watched them roll down the slope. They watched them roll past.

" 'Hey!' said the young Wise Guy. 'Now there's the way to get places! Why don't we use things like those?'

"The Wise Man gave him a look. 'Don't be a darn fool!' he said. 'That's just a gadget. It would never work as well as a mat does. Stick to the old ways, I say! They're the best.'

"The others agreed with the Wise Man. Well, the Wise Guy gave them an argument, and pretty soon they picked up clubs and settled his hash then and there. And would you believe it, another hundred thousand years went by before another man finally got the idea and made a wheel? I don't like to knock your ancestors, but of all the slow learners and dropouts. . . ."

"What do you mean, dropouts?"

"Your first ancestors," said Bronson, "were dropouts from trees. Well, now, here we are at last," he added, as a bridge finally came into sight.

It was a good big one, so I said, "Why don't you just walk across?"

But he shook his head.

"No, thank you, I'll swim. I'm not interested in getting caught in the middle of a bridge with a trailer truck coming. How do you think I've lived so long?"

His point was well taken, of course. He let me off near the bridge, and I started walking. It was a long, high bridge. Part way across I stopped to watch him swimming the river. He was sculling along, using his tail as a sweep, and making very good time. A couple of men were sitting near me on a scaffold, painting the bridge's steelwork.

"Whatcha looking at, sonny?" asked one of them.

"I'm watching a dinosaur swim the river," I said, and pointed. "See him?"

The painter looked down and nodded solemnly.

"Say, he's a big one, ain't he?" he said.

"He sure is. I was going to ride across on his back, but I would have gotten too wet."

"Oh, you bet you would have," said the painter, chuckling the way grown-ups do when they talk nonsense to children.

"Well, I have to go now," I said. "I have to get on him again and ride him to New York City."

"Have a good trip," said the other painter, and they both laughed.

When I reached the other side of the bridge, Bronson was waiting for me on top of an embankment alongside the highway. He was shaking himself off, but he was still pretty wet.

"Say, I'll need something to sit on for a while, till you dry off, or I'll get my pants soaked," I said.

"There're some haystacks in that field down there." Bronson pointed his head in their direction. "Climb aboard, but don't sit down. We'll go down there and I'll lift you up a mouthful of hay."

I turned and looked back at the men painting the bridge. They were watching me, so I waved to them and then stepped onto Bronson's tail.

"That'll give them something to think about," I said.

"Oh no, it won't," said Bronson. "They'll just decide it was a trick of the light, or that you suddenly jumped down the embankment on the other side. They'll think of some good explanation—anything but the right one."

Down in the hay field, Bronson picked a big mouthful of hay off a haystack and lifted it up to me. At the same time, he was swishing his tail around rather carelessly, and it happened to hit another haystack.

"Hey, watch that tail!" I said. "You just knocked a haystack to smithereens."

Bronson twisted his neck around to look, and his eyes took on a mischievous glint.

"You mean, like that?" he asked, and swished his tail through another haystack. It looked for all the

68

world as if it had exploded. Hay went flying every which way.

"That's fun!" he said, and squared away on another haystack. But this time when his tail swished through it, he let out a bellow you could have heard clear to New York City, if you could have heard it.

"Ow!" bellowed Bronson. "Something got me!"

By then I could see what was the matter.

"There was a pitchfork in that haystack," I reported. "Hold still! I'll go down and pull it out of your tail."

I scrambled down on my errand of mercy. Bronson had really got it good. It was all I could do to pull that pitchfork loose, and when I did, I could see he was bleeding.

"Bronson, this is serious," I said. "You could get a bad case of tetanus from a pitchfork wound."

"You mean, lockjaw?" he said, and there was a definite quaver in his voice. Bronson was scared.

"That's right. We've got to find the nearest drugstore in a hurry, so I can get some iodine to put on that wound."

"Iodine?" said Bronson. "What's iodine? I've never had any occasion to use it."

"It stops bleeding and prevents infection," I said. "Leave it to me. Let's see, where's the nearest town?"

We looked around and saw that we were not far from a village. I climbed up and sat down on my straw.

"Okay, get moving," I said. I certainly didn't want to have a sick dinosaur on my hands.

Bronson galloped into the village, where fortunately traffic was not too heavy. It was one of those neat Connecticut towns with a village green in the middle of it and quaint Ye Olde This and Ye Olde That Shoppes around the square. All very Early American. While Bronson waited on the green, I hurried over to Ye Olde Village Chemist Shoppe, which was the local drugstore.

"What can I do for you, sonny?" asked the druggist.

"I'd like a quart of iodine," I said breathlessly, and his eyebrows flew up.

"A *quart?*" he said. "What's happened, a railroad accident?"

"Naw, it's supplies for our football team."

"You boys must lose a lot of games," he said, and took down a bottle.

"I'd like a roll of the widest bandage material you have, too," I told him.

"This is the widest I've got," he said, producing a jumbo package and looking at me curiously.

"Fat boy," I explained, feeling I had to say something.

A minute later I was over on the village green again. A few people were walking around near us, so I moseyed behind a tree to do my disappearing act, not wanting to startle anyone. And when I spoke to Bronson, I should have whispered, because at that point, don't forget, anybody else could have heard me speak. In fact, someone else did. One of those sharp-faced women who always seem to hear everything was passing by just as I said to Bronson, "Psst! Shove your tail over here!"

She stopped, gasping indignantly.

"What did you say?" she squawked. By that time Bronson had shoved his tail my way.

"Watch where you step," he said. "It's sore!"

I scrambled aboard just as the woman decided to come over to where I was hiding and give me a piece of her mind. We left her looking all around for me.

Bronson hurried out of the village. I kept an eye out for an open field—a big one—and as soon as one came into sight I told him to get into the field, where no one would bother us. I climbed down with my supplies and took the rubber stopper out of the bottle. Bronson was looking around at it worriedly.

"Is that the iodine?"

"Yep. Hold still while I put it on," I said.

And with that I poured iodine all over his pitchfork wound.

7.

Ever see a dinosaur do a tap dance?

I was right about choosing a big field to stop in. Bronson needed plenty of room. When that iodine sank in, he practically stood on his tail for a second or two while he let out the loudest dinosaur roar I'll probably ever hear.

"YOWIE!" roared Bronson, and began stamping around the field like—well, you know how iodine feels. He really did some fancy steps for about two minutes there, and when he stopped he laid his head flat on the ground, panting.

He glared at me.

"You little monster!"

72

"Bronson, it's for your own good," I told him. "You won't get any lockjaw now."

"Well, I should think not!" he snorted, blowing up a dust cloud that looked like a small tornado.

I unwrapped the roll of gauze.

"Now, let me just get a bandage on that, and we'll be all set."

I put turn after turn of the white gauze around his tail, and finished it off in a nice big bow.

"There you are, all ready for a birthday party," I said, standing back to admire my work.

"You think you're pretty funny, don't you?" he said hotly, but he couldn't deny that I had done a neat job. By then the iodine was beginning to simmer down, and he was feeling better, anyway. I climbed up on his back and was glad to find that all his exercise had dried him off nicely.

"Wow! Believe me, I haven't been through anything like *that*," said Bronson, "since the first time I visited Yellowstone National Park. Of course, it wasn't a national park then, it was just a place I came across in my rambles. In fact, I may have been the first tourist that ever visited the area."

"What happened to you there?"

"Well, after a while I came across a lot of crusty patches of bare ground. I noticed a good-sized hole in the center of one of them. I was just examining the hole when not far away I heard a terrific rumble and a whoosh. I swung around for a look and saw a spout of water shooting into the air a couple of hundred feet high."

"A geyser, huh?"

"That's right, it was a geyser. Well, I was so amazed that I didn't pay attention to the rumbling that was beginning right under my feet. Now, as luck would have it, I'd swung my tail squarely over that hole. All at once a column of water shot up and all but took my tail off. And that water was hot!"

"I can well imagine," I said.

"I started to run, and that was my second mistake. I ran straight into some mud pots and got the worst hotfoot of my life. When I finally made it to firm ground I kept on running till I found a lake to cool off in, and I didn't come out of it for two days!"

"What happened when you came out?"

"Listen, I tiptoed out of that crazy park watching my step every inch of the way, and I never went back again for several million years. I wouldn't go near it till the park rangers had put up signs everywhere and I could tell what to watch out for. I've always been a great sightseer, but to this day the world's most famous geyser is not one of my favorite sights."

"You mean to say . . . ?"

"That's right. With the whole Wide Open Spaces around me, I had to get my tail in the way of Old Faithful!"

We made good time for a while, until we came to another big river and had to find a bridge again. Meanwhile, I was planning ahead, thinking about the night we were going to spend in Central Park.

"While we're near a town, I'd better buy myself that sleeping bag," I said.

"Good idea. Let's keep an eye out for a shopping center with a sporting goods store."

An unpleasant possibility occurred to me. I checked my wallet.

"Say, I don't have enough money with me to buy a sleeping bag!"

"Hmm," said Bronson. "Well, we'll have to do something about that. I'll give it some thought while I'm swimming the river."

When we met on the other side, once again I had a wet dinosaur to contend with, but fortunately there was some straw spread on a new embankment beside the bridge. I gathered some of that to take up onto Bronson with me, and he picked up some to munch on.

"Now, about our money problems," he said, chewing thoughtfully on a long piece of straw while I was taking the wet bandage off his tail and putting on a fresh one. "I'll bet some loan shark has an office along the waterfront here, if we look. You know how those crooks work, lending money to poor people and then making them pay back twice as much."

I was surprised at Bronson, with all his IQ, coming up with such an unrealistic idea.

"What are you talking about?" I said. "You don't think a loan shark is going to lend money to a ten-year-old kid, do you?"

"Who said anything about lending it?" asked Bronson, with a wink. "Try this for size. We find one of those bloodsuckers alone in his office. You walk in and leave the door open. He asks what you want. You give him a fresh answer that makes him jump up to chase you out. When he gets to the door, I bop him one on the head with my chin. You take a few bucks out of his pocket, and we're all set. Regular Robin Hood stuff, robbing the rich to give to the poor."

"What do you mean, the poor?"

"Well . . . you can give the sleeping bag to some poor kid when we're through with it."

I was relieved to find that Bronson still had his thinking cap on, but I shook my head.

"Bronson, you're tempting me. I'd love every minute of that caper. But we can't do it," I said. "I don't like to be stuffy, but all the same, two wrongs don't make a right."

Bronson picked up another piece of straw and chewed on it reflectively for a moment. Then he sighed.

"No, I suppose not. For that matter, I suppose it isn't fair to bop somebody who can't see you, except in self-defense," he said. "Well, have you got a better idea?"

I didn't have, until then, but suddenly I thought of something.

"Wait a minute," I said, and pulled the road map out of my pocket. I studied it for a minute, and nodded. "Why not? Listen, I've got a friend who has a country place not far from here, practically on our way, and he's in Europe right now. I got a postcard from him yesterday. Now, I know he's done a lot of camping. . . . The only thing is, I wonder if we can get into his house?"

Bronson chuckled confidently.

"Show me the lock I can't pick," he said.

"You mean it?"

"Try me. All I need is a piece of wire."

"Bronson, you're a wonder. Let me just check my job on your bandage, and then we'll go."

He swung his head around to inspect my work.

"You might have left off the bow this time. It looks so silly," he grumbled, but I said, "What do you care? Nobody can see you."

We stopped by a town dump and found a piece of wire. When we reached my friend's house, I followed Bronson's instructions as to how to bend the wire. Then, holding the wire with his teeth, he stuck one end in the keyhole, and his big eyes rolled this way and that as he felt around inside the lock. You talk about delicate technique—he was an artist. In about five seconds there was a click, and I was able to open the door.

Bronson spit out the wire and said, "I hope you'll be able to find his camping stuff, after we've gone to all this trouble."

"Don't worry about that. This guy is one of those orderly people who have a place for everything and everything in its place. You'll see. Everything will be labeled."

"I'll watch through the basement windows."

It gave me a funny feeling to go sneaking into a friend's house, but I tried not to let it bother me. I went out to the kitchen and down the stairs, and sure enough his basement did not disappoint me. Every box and trunk was neatly labeled, and one trunk was marked, "Camping Equipment."

Neat, orderly people always go too far, though. The trunk was not only labeled, it was locked.

I hate to tell you all the fuss we had to go to. How I had to open a basement window so Bronson could stick his head in, and then run up and get the wire again, and then run down and push the trunk over close enough so he could pick the lock. If anyone could have seen him outside that house with his head stuck in the basement window, it would have been quite a sight. He looked like the world's largest ostrich.

By the time we finished we had both had a workout, but I had a nice sleeping bag to show for it. I closed the window and shoved the trunk back to its place and shut the front door and stuck the wire in a tree so we could use it again when we came back, and we were ready to go.

A few miles rolled by with more comfort than ever, now that I had a sleeping bag to sit on. I wouldn't have had a care in the world, if I hadn't started thinking about how heavy the traffic gets down around New York, and in the city.

"Bronson, how are we going to get into town?" I asked finally. "I don't see how you can maneuver around all those cars and people."

He nodded his big head.

"You're right about that, but don't worry, my bag of tricks isn't empty yet. As a matter of fact, I've just been thinking about that, wondering how to break the news to you."

"Break what news to me?"

We were crossing a field. Bronson pulled up and glanced around at me.

"The way we're going to make the last leg of our trip," he said. "I hope you won't be scared, because there's nothing to be scared about."

By now, of course, my curiosity was at fever pitch.

"Stop beating around the bush," I said. "Tell me what's up."

"*We're* going to be up, that's what," he said. "You

see, I've worked out this system for filtering hydrogen out of the air I take into my lungs. What I do is, I pump the hydrogen into my body cavities, and the first thing you know, I'm airborne."

Airborne! If Bronson had searched through the biggest dictionary he could find for a word to scare me with, he couldn't have come up with a better one than that.

"Bronson!" I cried. "For Pete's sake, I've never flown in my life!"

"No? Then it's high time you did. In fact, we might as well take off right now, before we start running into a lot of suburban traffic."

"But I'm scared to death of planes!"

"So am I. We'll stay away from them," said Bronson, misunderstanding me, or pretending to. "Listen, when you fly with me you haven't a thing to worry about."

As you may have guessed by now, I had been pretty much of a timid soul all my life. I'll admit it. But now, for some reason, a little throb of courage ran through me and thawed out some of my fright. I was still scared, but at the same time I suddenly knew I wouldn't miss a chance like this if it killed me.

"Well. . . ." I said.

"Well what, Tad?"

"Well, I've come this far, I might as well go all the way," I said. "Are you sure I'll be safe?"

"Positive. Actually, it's the way Lem and I travel most of the time, though he's not too fond of air travel because it gets pretty cold up there. He always wears his long underwear, and takes enough blankets for an army. You'd better get inside that sleeping bag before we take off."

I took a deep breath.

"Okay," I said, and rolled it out. While I was slipping inside and zipping it up so that only my head and shoulders and arms were outside, I noticed that Bronson seemed to be swelling up.

"You're pumping hydrogen, huh?" I said.

"Yup," he grunted—it was obviously quite a physical effort. All at once the ground seemed to float away under us, and the next thing I knew I was looking down at neat green fields and toy houses.

I was filled with such admiration that I didn't even feel terrified.

"Bronson, I don't know anything about flying," I said, "but I don't see how a take-off could be any smoother than that."

"Thank you, Tad," said Bronson, sincerely flattered. "I had to work on it for quite a while before I got the knack, believe you me. I wish you could have seen me the first time I tried it. I bounced around like a rubber ball. Of course, the tail motion is the whole thing," he added, and looking back I saw the way he was swishing his tail from side to side in a smooth movement that controlled our flight and gave us our propulsion.

"Looks a lot like your swimming stroke," I said.

"Practically the same," he said. "A little more tip action, maybe, but otherwise very much the same."

It is hard to describe the sensation of flying a dinosaur to someone who has never flown one. Of course, I wasn't really flying Bronson, but he let me pretend I was. I'd bang down my right fist, and he'd bank gently to the right. Then I'd bang my left and he'd bank to the left. It was a great time of day for a flight, too, because it was getting on toward dusk, and down below us the lights were just beginning to come on. Ahead in the distance I could make out the skyline of New York City, with thousands of pinpricks of light twinkling up and down the skyscrapers.

"Bronson, I wouldn't have missed this for anything in the world!" I said. For someone like me who had never flown before, it was the greatest thrill imaginable. Instead of being scared, I made a marvelous discovery. I loved flying!

"No, sir!" I said, "I wouldn't have missed——"

And suddenly I was missing.

The trouble was, I got careless, and leaned the wrong way just as Bronson was banking. I fell off into space in my sleeping bag.

And a sleeping bag is no parachute!

8.

Falling through space is the dreamiest sensation I have ever had, because you don't feel as if you are falling. You simply feel as if you are floating.

At the same time, I knew very well that some hard, hard ground was rushing up to meet me. I was never more frightened in my life.

"Bronson!" I screamed, and I remember wondering whether Charlie and Sarah would ever find out why I had disappeared. Would they ever connect my disappearance with a body that fell out of the sky down near New York City?

A huge shape dived past me and shot under me. I hit with a thump that knocked the breath out of me.

I was back on Bronson.

"Bronson!" I cried. There was no time for an exchange of comment, however, because we were not out of the woods yet. In fact, we were almost *in* the woods. We were very low, and Bronson was dodging trees and rooftops and television antennas as fast as he could dodge.

Right away I realized what the trouble was, because I could hear him pumping away desperately. In order to dive down under me, Bronson had released a lot of hydrogen in a hurry. Now he was struggling to stay airborne and work his hydrogen level back up to where it should be.

For a couple of hair-raising minutes it was touch and go. The way he maneuvered his seventy feet of neck and body and tail would have been a credit to a Flying Circus ace. And gradually he gained altitude, until finally we rose clear of even the tallest television tower and could breathe easily again.

"Bronson, I want to thank you," I said in a trembling voice.

"Forget it," he said. "All in a day's work. I've never lost a passenger yet."

But just the same, I was impressed. Bronson had risked his life for me—and when someone who is millions of years old does that for you, you can't help but feel pretty special! And very grateful.

From then on I stayed flat on my belly, and we had no more trouble.

Luckily a breeze was blowing most of the smog away from over New York that evening. We had an absolutely spectacular view of the skyline as we came in over the city. When Bronson suggested we take a turn over the midtown section, I was all for it.

Radio City was a great sight, of course, and over in the Hudson River we could see all the big ocean liners tied up at the piers. But the best sight of all was the Empire State Building, when Bronson slowly circled around it. A lot of people were up in the observation tower, taking advantage of the fine evening.

"Hey, look at us!" I shouted at them. "Get your money's worth!"

"They don't know what they're missing," said Bronson.

"It seems a shame," I said. "We're the greatest sight New York has ever seen, and nobody can see us. How about grabbing hold of the top of the Empire State Building for a minute? You wouldn't be the first blimp that ever used it for a mooring, you know."

"Nothing doing," said Bronson. "Look at what happened to King Kong when *he* climbed up on the Empire State Building."

"For Pete's sake! Do you mean to say you saw that movie?"

"Certainly," said Bronson. "I go to drive-in movies all the time. I saw King Kong on a triple bill with two

86

other science-fiction movies. The other two were un-
believable."

"Come to think of it, it must have been a great thing
for you when drive-in movies started."

"It certainly was. I generally go to them a couple of
times a week."

After a while we decided we had better get uptown
and pick out our campsite. It was almost dark when
we touched down in Central Park, in the middle of
one of the meadows. It was a pleasure to see the way
Bronson came in for a landing, slowly releasing his hydrogen until finally he made a four-footed landing as
light as a feather. Nobody was in sight in any direction.
Most people stayed out of the park after dark. Bronson walked me over to the Central Park West entrance
at 100th Street, and waited for me while I ran to the
nearest grocery store to pick up the marshmallows and
a few other things that looked good to me, like hot
dogs and pickles and potato chips. I was hungry again.
For that matter, I went into two or three stores. I had
the strangest cravings for things like jelly beans and
frosted cookies and cinnamon drops—stuff I hadn't
bothered with for years and years.

"I'll have a snack myself," said Bronson, before I
left. "If they have any nice-looking Boston lettuce,
bring me five or six heads."

Back in the park, we went up to the far end, where

87

there is a hollow, so that we could keep our campfire out of sight. I gorged myself, and Bronson seemed to enjoy his lettuce. For that matter, he even had a pickle, just to make an occasion out of it.

We had a perfect night for our outing, just nippy enough to make a fire feel good. I must admit it was great to be a boy again and sit around a campfire with a dinosaur like Bronson, cracking jokes and singing songs. Bronson knew them all. The best moment, however, was when Bronson burped. What a burp *that* was!

"Excuse me," he said. "It's that pickle."

We had a regular jamboree. Bronson told stories about how he helped Newton think of the law of gravity by having an apple fall on his head ("How did you think that apple happened to fall? Somebody had to shake the tree!") and about the time he invented skiing during the Ice Age ("I used to ski a lot, before the slopes got so crowded"). After a while, however, I was having trouble keeping my eyes open. Bronson chuckled.

"Bedtime for little boys," he commented. "We'd better turn in, because tomorrow's the big day."

I was too sleepy to argue. But just as I was settling down in my sleeping bag, I sat up again.

"Hey, Bronson, I just remembered something. To-morrow's Sunday, and the museum doesn't open till one o'clock."

"Hmm," said Bronson sleepily. "That's all right."

I began to think about the museum, and worried myself wide awake.

"I still don't see how you're ever going to get inside," I said, but got no answer. Bronson was already asleep.

9.

In the morning Bronson had me up at six o'clock. He wanted to make the most of our time, before we went to the museum.

I finished off the marshmallows for breakfast, much to my own surprise. Ordinarily I couldn't have looked a marshmallow in the face at that hour.

"Well, this has been quite an experience," I said, gazing around us. "When do you suppose was the last time a dinosaur was in Central Park?"

"Never," said Bronson. "Back in our day, this Manhattan Island that New York is built on was under water."

"You mean it? Then this is a first!"

"It sure is. Maybe a last, too. Who knows?"

We flew downtown to the tip of Manhattan Island,

had a look at the Statue of Liberty, and took a walk through the financial district. It's very quiet down there on Sundays, with no traffic at all. As we stood in Wall Street, looking at an old building, Bronson pointed out a plaque on the wall.

"This is where George Washington became your first president and made his inaugural speech back in 1789. I wish I could have heard him, but I was in Australia that year, studying the bushmen. They're remarkable, you know. Straight out of the Stone Age, as you call it."

"You must have flown all over the world," I said enviously.

"Yes, indeed. Why, I flew the Atlantic a million years before Lindbergh even *thought* of it."

"You've had an interesting life, Bronson."

"Yes, I have," he agreed. "It's had its ups and downs, but on the whole I can't complain."

Well, the morning went fast, and the first thing we knew it was noon. When we got back uptown there were quite a few people strolling through the park, enjoying a fine fall day. I got off Bronson behind a tree and stared up at him. He had never looked bigger than he did at that moment, when I stood there thinking about the museum doors.

"Bronson, I'll be honest with you," I said, "I'm worried. I don't think you realize what you're up against, when it comes to getting into the museum."

"Oh yes, I do," he said.

"All right, then, just how do you think you're going to manage it?"

"Brace yourself," said Bronson. "Now you're *really* going to see something. I'm about to do my famous squeeze down. It's the most difficult thing I do, and it must be quite a sight. I've often wished there was a mirror large enough to watch myself do it in. But anyway, here goes!"

I thought I had already seen just about everything, but what happened now beat all the rest. Bronson started to grunt and suck in his breath, and right before my eyes he began to shrink.

He got smaller and smaller and smaller. Seventy feet, sixty feet, fifty feet—twenty feet!

Ten feet!

At ten feet he was pretty red in the face from the effort.

"Wow!" he said, breathing hard. "Well, that's it. Let me tell you, I wouldn't want to do *that* every day of my life! I can't tell you how many million years it took me to work out a stunt like this one. Needless to say, I only use it in real emergencies."

If I hadn't been used to marvels by now, I would probably have fainted again, the way I did when I first saw him. Even as it was, I had to sit down for a minute till my head cleared. I was overcome with admiration.

I realized now that I was in the presence of one of the greatest geniuses of all time, if not *the* greatest.

"Well, that certainly is one way of handling the situation," I said. "How long can you hold it?"

"Smart boy!" said Bronson, pleased with me. "You've put your finger squarely on the difficulty!"

"Well, it's obvious that you're making quite an effort," I said modestly, but I don't mind admitting I was flattered to receive such an accolade.

"I can only squeeze down for about an hour at a time, so we'd better get cracking," said Bronson. "What time is it?"

"Ten minutes till one."

"Let's go."

When we reached the broad front steps of the museum, my heart sank.

"Bronson! Look at those doors!" I groaned.

I had forgotten what kind of doors the museum had. Revolving doors!

"Never mind," said Bronson. "Come on."

"But how are you ever going to get through a revolving door? There may be only ten feet of you now, but ten feet is too much for one of those things."

"Where there's a will, there's a way," said Bronson, and walked on ahead up to one of the tall, narrow doors. Swinging his tail forward on the ground, he stepped over it with one hind leg, so that it was under him. Then he stood up on his hind legs, held his tail against his chest with his front legs, and waddled into the revolving door like an old lady carrying a sack of groceries. He pushed his way inside as neatly as could be. He was straightening out his tail with a smug expression on his face when I came through. I wanted to compliment him on one more great performance in the clutch, but two guards who were talking to each other near the entrance glanced around, and I remembered that other people could hear me now.

"Can you tell me how to get to the dinosaur exhibit, please?" I asked one of the guards.

He glanced down my way with a chuckle.

"It beats me how these kids all want to see the dinosaurs," he said. "Of course, they're interesting, but don't be forgetting, sonny, they weren't very smart. Take bears, now. Your average bear could think rings around your average dinosaur any day in the week."

"Sure," said the other guard, "and your average chimp could make a monkey out of him."

Needless to say, none of this talk sat very well with Bronson. I was conscious of him fuming at my elbow all the time the guards were talking.

"Well, anyway, if you want to see the dinosaurs, sonny, you'll have to go to the top floor," said the first guard. "The fourth floor, that is. You can take the elevator, or the stairs to your left."

When we started on, Bronson gave them two or three dirty looks over his shoulder.

"Bears!" he said. "Chimps!"

"Well, now, Bronson, you've got to admit that your average dinosaur was no egghead," I whispered, trying to smooth things over. "You're an exception."

"Maybe so," he snapped, "but we still don't have to take that kind of talk!" He made an obvious effort to get hold of himself. "Oh, well, you get all kinds in this world, and I'm not going to let them spoil my day."

One problem for Bronson, of course, was to keep from bumping into people and scaring them to death, but he managed with a skill born of long experience. Fortunately, there were not many other visitors in the museum yet, and it is so enormous it can take lots of them without seeming crowded.

We used the stairs, of course. They were nice wide ones that gave Bronson ample room to operate in. When we reached the top floor, another guard happened to be walking past.

"Ask him where we'll find the brontosaurus," said Bronson, and I did.

"Right around the corner in the main hall," said the guard. We hurried along the corridor—and suddenly there it was, in front of us. Best of all, we had the hall to ourselves.

Well, if you ever saw an excited little dinosaur, it was Bronson. There, in the center of that great hall, stood the mounted skeletons of three dinosaurs, an allosaurus, a stegosaurus, and a brontosaurus. There was no doubt that the brontosaurus was by far the largest.

Bronson walked round and round the tremendous skeleton. He was understandably fascinated.

"I wonder if I knew him."

"That's hard to say, I suppose. Not much to go on."

He shook his head reflectively.

"Amazing to realize that's what my bones look like. Makes a fellow stop and think."

He frowned at the other skeletons in the central exhibit.

"Can't say much for their taste here. I didn't mind the stegosauruses, they were decent enough in their way, but I could have done without being reminded of that nasty meat-eater," he said, jerking his head at the allosaurus.

"Here's some information about him," I said, looking at a description in a big frame on the wall. "It says the allosaurus was a large, aggressive hunter that probably preyed upon plant-eating dinosaurs just as modern lions prey upon antelopes in Africa."

"Antelopes!" said Bronson indignantly. "What a comparison!"

"It also says that the gigantic brontosauruses were inoffensive plant-eaters that lived in the swamps, rivers, and lakes of late Jurassic times, feeding upon the lush vegetation that grew in such environments. How does that sound?"

"Pretty fair guesswork," conceded Bronson. "Accurate, on the whole. We certainly *tried* not to offend anybody."

He joined me at the wall cabinet and nodded his head toward the skeleton of a camptosaurus, a small dinosaur hardly more than six feet long, standing in the case.

"Well, I'm glad to see they have some of the little chaps here, too," he said. "Most of you human beings, except ones like Lem who have really made a study of us, seem to think that all dinosaurs were big ones like me. I mean, like I usually am. The truth is, of course, that many dinosaurs were small fry no more than six feet long. The tyrannosauruses considered some of them nothing more than appetizers," he said, shuddering. "Something to eat on a cracker. They used to snap them up in a single bite."

"I noticed there was another hall to the left of the stairs when we came up," I told him. "The sign said, 'Cretaceous Dinosaurs.' Want to have a look?"

"Cretaceous, eh? That's the later bunch. Sure, while we're here, let's see them all."

When we got there, however, Bronson was not so sure he was glad we had come. Because there, rearing up ferociously in the center of the room, was the skeleton of a tyrannosaurus, largest of the meat-eaters. Bronson started at the sight of him.

"Look at those jaws! Look at those teeth!" he said. "I ask you! Did you ever see anything as ugly in your life? I wish I had my full size back—I'd love to give him one good swift kick!"

I could just imagine giant bones clattering all over the room, and guards running from everywhere.

"Easy, Bronson. Let bygones be bygones," I said. "Let's go back to the other hall."

"Oh, very well," he said, "but when I look at that big creep, it seems like yesterday. . . . Did I ever show you my scar, where one almost got me? I did a swan dive off a high cliff into the water just in the nick of time, let me tell you! That was a splash the world didn't soon forget!"

I managed to get him out of there and back into the other hall, and he began to enjoy himself again. It was an education to be there with Bronson and hear his comments on the various exhibits. Everything was going great until a tall, thin, fussy-looking man came in with about twenty boys following him. They were more or less my size, about ten or eleven years old. He led them straight to the brontosaurus skeleton.

"I want to hear this," said Bronson, so we walked over and stationed ourselves beside the man to listen. As we came up, he had bent down to one of the boys who was asking him a question. We heard the boy call him Professor Prinny.

"We'll all stop there on the way out," Professor Prinny told the boy, "but right now we're going to learn about the dinosaurs."

He straightened up and clapped his hands for attention.

"Now, then, boys, here we have the brontosaurus, one of the largest dinosaurs that ever lived," he said, waving his hand at the skeleton. "It belongs to a suborder of the saurichian dinosaurs known as the sauropods, which means 'lizard-footed.' "

"So far, so good," said Bronson, nodding agreement, and holding up one foot for me to inspect.

"It was exceeded in size only by the diplodocus," the professor went on, "and by the brachiosaurus, largest of them all."

"Oh, him!" said Bronson jealously. "Silly-looking creature. Built like a giraffe, he was."

"The brachiosaurus was not so long as the brontosaurus or the diplodocus," continued Professor Prinny, "but it was very bulky."

"Why beat around the bush?" said Bronson. "He was a slob!"

Professor Prinny turned his attention back to the brontosaurus.

"The brontosaurus was a vegetarian. Its teeth were not sharp, but were flat, like blocks or pegs, so that it could chew up leaves and other vegetable matter," he said, and Bronson gapped his mouth open in my face to give me a look at his teeth. The professor was quite right.

"This one, as you can see from the sign, was sixty-seven feet in length and may have weighed thirty tons when alive. Considering how small its head and mouth were, in relation to its vast size," he continued, "it is surprising that the brontosaurus managed to eat enough to provide nourishment for its enormous body."

"It wasn't easy, bub," said Bronson, again nodding agreement, though of course the man could not see or hear him.

If the professor had only known enough to quit when he was ahead of the game, everything would have been fine. But now he got onto dangerous ground.

"For all their size, however," he said, "the giant dinosaurs had very little intelligence. They were not only the largest animals that ever lived, but also some of the stupidest."

That really brought Bronson's head up. He glared at the speaker in no uncertain fashion. I began to get nervous. I wished I could have tugged at Professor Prinny's sleeve and said, "Mister, I've got a friend here who doesn't take kindly to nasty cracks about dinosaurs, so watch it," but of course I couldn't. He wouldn't have understood. I had to stand there helplessly while he added more fuel to the fire.

"The dinosaurs had such tiny brains that they hardly knew what was going on. They moved around more like automatons or robots than living, intelligent animals."

If looks could kill, Professor Prinny would have

dropped dead. If only he could have known that a real live dinosaur was standing at his elbow, I'm sure he would have changed his tune in a hurry. Bronson's eyes were flashing, and I didn't like the way he was looking at the professor's leg. For an inoffensive plant-eater, his expression was misleading.

"Bronson, don't let him bug you," I whispered, but I was too late. All at once Bronson reached out and gave poor old Prinny a good nip on the thigh.

"Ow!" cried the professor, and leaped straight up into the air. When he came down, he glared around in our direction, and of course all he saw there was me.

It was no time for explanations.

"Come on!" I said to Bronson, and we started running.

"Get him!" yelled one of the boys, and right away all twenty of them were after us. Bronson flipped his tail around behind us and tripped up the front four or five. That gave us time to get into the corridor.

"Jump on!" said Bronson. When the boys poured out behind us, they stared around angrily. Because of course the instant I jumped on Bronson, I disappeared.

"He's gone!" said one.

"He must have ducked around the corner!" said another. "Let's find him!"

But by then we were galloping away down the stairs. Bronson was a perfect size for me now, small enough so that I could hang onto his neck.

"This is great!" I told him. "Our worries are over."

"That's what you think," said Bronson, glancing back at me. At first I thought he was just red in the face from the exertion. But then with a jolt I guessed what the trouble was.

"Bronson!" I cried, scared out of my wits. "Don't tell me!"

He nodded.

"We've got to get out of here," he said grimly. "I can't hold myself in much longer."

Now I was dizzy with fright.

"Good grief!" I moaned. "Head for the exit!"

Well, you know how it is when you're trying to get out of a huge building in a hurry. Down the endless stairs raced Bronson, skidding around corners, swerving to avoid people, sliding to a stop at dead ends, scrambling and slipping on the marble floors. It was like riding a time bomb. Every foot of the way I had a vision of him suddenly swelling up into a seventy-foot monster and cracking the walls and sending the whole enormous building full of stuffed elephants and tigers and gorillas and bottlenosed whales tumbling down on our heads.

Just when I had given up and was riding along with my eyes shut, waiting to go through the ceiling, Bronson rounded a corner and I opened one eye. There ahead of us across the vast entrance hall were the revolving doors. Bronson did that last stretch like a dinosaur greyhound, and slammed to a stop in front of them.

"Jump off!" he cried, and a small boy suddenly appeared out of thin air, if anyone had cared to watch. Fortunately, nobody happened to be looking directly my way just then, or that person would have gotten quite a shock. Bronson reared up on his hind legs and rushed into a revolving door. The only trouble was, in his haste he forgot his tail.

"Ow!" roared Bronson. The end of his tail with the bow on it was caught in the door, right where it was sore. But there was no time for sympathy. I grabbed it and stuffed it inside the revolving door with him, and he stumbled on through. I pushed through behind him and leaped on his back. Bronson shot down the broad front steps and ripped across the street missing cars by an eyelash. We had hardly got inside the park before I felt as though I were riding a fast elevator in a modern office building, the kind that leaves your stomach on the first floor.

"Whew!" said Bronson, full size again. "Does that feel good!"

10.

We had an easy flight back to Rhode Island. Even with a couple of rest stops, and with stopping to return the sleeping bag, we made good time, and touched down just as it was getting along toward dusk. There was the woodshed, with the big rock still in place in front of it. Bronson nosed the rock out of the way. I backed my car out, and he put his foot on it to bring it back to normal size.

"Now, how about me?" I said.

"You're sure you don't want to keep on being a boy?"

I sighed.

"I almost wish I could, but it's impossible. No, I guess I'll have to pick up where I left off."

"Cousin Charlie, and all that?"

I made a face, but I nodded.

"I guess so."

"All right, then. A bargain is a bargain," said Bronson. And with that, he lifted his foot and rested it lightly on my head. When he took it away, I was a middle-aged man again.

Of course, we had both forgotten about my wallet. Now I had the biggest dollar bills anybody ever saw. After we had taken a look at a king-sized George Washington and had a good laugh about it, Bronson reduced my wallet to the proper size. Then we stood and looked at each other.

"Well, I guess that just about does it," I said.

Bronson looked away and shuffled his feet around.

"Yes, I guess it does," he said. "But I want to thank you for going down there with me. I enjoyed every minute of it, and I hope you did, too."

"I certainly did," I said, and stared down the hill at nothing in particular. "Mind if I walk you back to the pond?"

"I'd be honored," said Bronson. We started walking down the hill. Neither of us thought of anything to say till we reached the pond.

Then I said, "Well, I suppose you and Lem will be heading south now."

Bronson nodded.

"Yes. I'll pick him up in the morning."

I stared down at a pebble I was pushing around aimlessly with the toe of my sneaker.

"I don't suppose I'll ever see you again," I said.

Bronson shrugged one of those sizable shrugs of his.

"Who knows?" he said. "You never can tell, in this life. And by the way, that shot with the Inviso-Ray gun may do wonders for you. Take Lem, now. He doesn't look a day older than he did when I met him nearly two hundred years ago."

My spine really came alive when he said that.

"What? Do you mean to say——"

Bronson nodded.

"Lem was with Washington at Valley Forge, and he was an old man then. An old farmer with a lot of fight left in him. He's quite a fellow, Lem is. Well, I suppose you're right, though. Back to Cousin Charlie and the plumbing."

"I guess so," I said. "I mean, what else can I do?"

"That's something you'll have to decide for yourself, Tad. Good luck," said Bronson, and waded abruptly into the pond. He turned around and nodded to me, then backed farther into the water and lowered his head, and as he did so, he seemed to fade.

By the time his head went out of sight, I couldn't be sure whether he had faded first, or disappeared first. All I know is that I turned around and walked away without being able to see very well where I was going.

It's a strange sensation when you feel your best friend is a seventy-foot dinosaur you'll never see again.

———————

I drove to Uncle Chester's, and got there just in time for supper.

"Well, how did the job go?" asked Cousin Charlie, the minute I came in.

The thought of sitting there and trying to explain things to the whole bunch of them was too much for me. So I put off the inevitable by using a sneaky technique.

"I had quite a weekend," I said, "but everything worked out all right."

"Well, that's good," he said. "I hope Wilson doesn't try to stick us with a big bill. I'm sure you did as much of the work as he did."

"I did every bit as much as he did," I agreed.

I watched Charlie clean his plate and take seconds of everything, with Aunt Lulie seeing to it as usual that her boy got the choice bits. For a sick man, Charlie had an amazingly healthy appetite, almost as good a one as his father. When we had finished, Uncle Chester set back puffing on a cigar so big it reminded me of Bronson's.

"We missed you, Tad," he said, "but I'm glad you took care of that plumbing before it got any worse."

Charlie sighed.

"I sure wish I'd been up to helping. I hate having to

push it all off on Tad—but I must say this weekend has done me a lot of good. I feel worlds better."

His mother gave him a worried look.

"Now, Charlie, don't you go and try to do too much, just because you feel better," she said. "You've got to save your strength."

"Don't worry, Mother, I will," said Charlie, and I was sure he meant it.

Not long after supper we started home. We hadn't gone far before a welcome sight made me slam on the brakes.

"Tad! What on earth is the matter?" cried Charlie.

"I want to check the back tires," I said, and got out.

A friend of mine was sitting alongside the road.

"Bronson!" I whispered. "How come I can see you again?"

"Because you wanted to," said Bronson.

I nodded thoughtfully.

"That's what I figured."

"I knew you'd be coming along here on your way home, so I walked over."

He looked me in the eye.

"Well?"

"Will Lem mind?"

"Not at all."

I nodded again. Then I climbed back in the car and told them everything was all right, and drove on home. All the way Cousin Charlie complained about the fright I had given him, stopping like that, and said I'd spoiled all the good the weekend had done him. When we got to the house, while they were getting out, I carried their bags to the front porch, but then I came back to the car.

"I've got to go see a friend," I told Charlie. He gave me a peevish look.

"Tad, you've been acting mighty strange this evening," he complained. "What's the matter with you?"

"Nothing," I said. "I never felt better in my life."

I watched them go to the front door, and watched him pick up a note I had already spotted there, stuck under the door. He held it out where he could read it. I'll never forget the look on his face when he turned around.

"Tad! Here's a note from Wilson! He says he came, and nobody was here!"

"That's right, Charlie," I said, "nobody was here."

I backed the car out of the drive, waved cheerily, and drove away.

About the Artist: Born in Bucharest, Romania, Mircea Vasiliu was already a published author at thirteen. After studying law, he joined the Diplomatic Corps and was sent to Washington, D.C. He resigned from his post after Communist encroachment of Romania and was granted asylum in the United States. After a variety of odd jobs, ranging from curtain salesman in a department store to legal researcher at the Library of Congress, he went back to art school and became a free-lance illustrator. He is author-illustrator of many children's books and has written two adult books as well.

About the Book: The text typeface is linotype Janson and the display typeface is Mistral. The book was printed by offset. Mr. Vasiliu's illustrations are pen and ink line drawings with a wash.